In memory of Our Doris, my fantastic mum,
and for Jane, wonderful mother of our children
—A.B.

SQUARE
FISH
An Imprint of Macmillan

Square Fish and the Square Fish logo are trademarks of Macmillan and
are used by Farrar Straus Giroux under license from Macmillan.

Library of Congress Cataloging-in-Publication Data
Browne, Anthony, date.
My mom / Anthony Browne.
p.   cm.
Summary: A child describes the many wonderful things about "my mom,"
who can make anything grow, roar like a lion, and be as comfy as an armchair.
ISBN 978-0-374-40026-2
[1. Mothers—Fiction. 2. Mother and child—Fiction.] I. Title.
PZ7.B81276My 2005   [E]–dc22   2004047173

Originally published in Great Britain by Doubleday, a division of Transworld Publishers
First published in the United States by Farrar Straus Giroux
First Square Fish Edition: September 2012
Square Fish logo designed by Filomena Tuosto
mackids.com

5 7 9 10 8 6 4

My Mom
Anthony Browne

SQUARE
FISH

FARRAR STRAUS GIROUX

New York

She's nice, my mom.

My mom's a fantastic cook,

and a brilliant juggler.

She's a great painter,

and the STRONGEST
woman in the world!

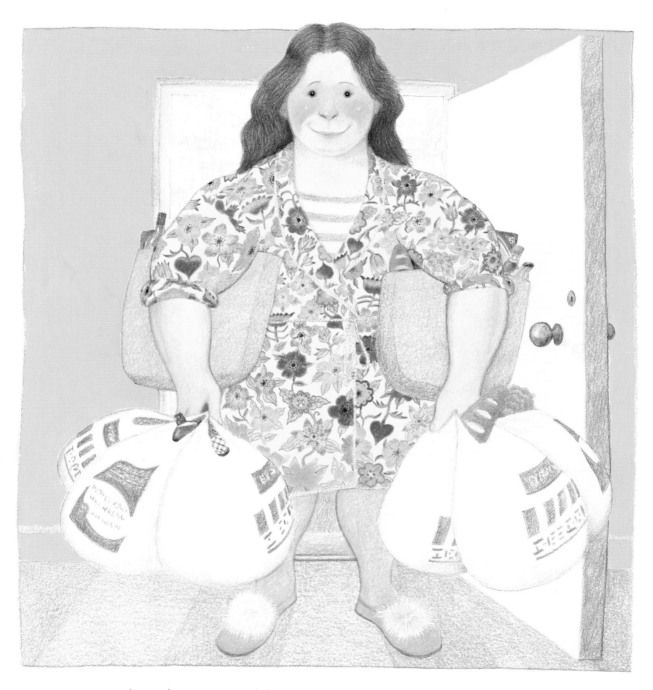

She's really nice, my mom.

My mom's a magic gardener;
she can make ANYTHING grow.

And she's a good fairy;
when I'm sad she can make me happy.

She can sing like an angel,

and roar like a lion.

She's really, REALLY nice, my mom.

My mom's as beautiful as a butterfly,

and as comfy
as an
armchair.

She's as soft as a kitten,

and as tough as a rhino.

She's really, REALLY,
REALLY nice, my mom.

My mom could be a dancer,

or an astronaut.

She could be a film star,

THE BOSS

or the big boss. But she's MY mom.

She's a SUPERMOM!

And she makes me laugh. A lot.

I love my mom.

And you know what?

SHE LOVES ME!

(And she always will.)

SHE LOVES ME!

(And she always will.)